KU-755-236

Contents

Billy

Sam

BOYS RULE!
Golf Legends

Felice Arena and Phil Kettle

illustrated by
Gus Gordon

RISING ★ STARS

First published in Great Britain by
RISING STARS UK LTD 2004
22 Grafton Street, London, W1S 4EX

Reprinted 2004, 2006, 2007

For information visit our website at:
www.risingstars-uk.com

British Library Cataloguing in Publication Data

A CIP record for this book is available from the British Library.

ISBN: 978-1-904591-70-2

First published in 2003 by
MACMILLAN EDUCATION AUSTRALIA PTY LTD
15–19 Claremont Street, South Yarra, Australia 3141

Visit our website at www.macmillan.com.au or
go directly to www.macmillanlibrary. com.au

Associated companies and representatives throughout the world.

Project Management by Limelight Press Pty Ltd
Cover and text design by Lore Foye
Illustrations by Gus Gordon

Printed in China

CHAPTER 1

The Plan

It's the weekend, and best friends,
Billy and Sam, have been watching
the golf on TV. They get bored with
Tiger Woods and decide to play their
own golf game, at the local park.

Sam "We can start from that flat
bit down at the park."
Billy "What'll we use for golf clubs?"

Sam "We can use Dad's. When he came home from golf last weekend, I heard him say he was never playing golf again. He said it was a stupid game and threw his golf clubs in the corner so I guess he won't be using them for a while."

Billy "Don't you think your old man will freak if we use his clubs?"

Sam "Well, he reckoned he was never playing golf again so I don't think so. He'll probably be glad his clubs will still get used."

The boys decide it might be safer to head for the park through the backyard. They pick up the clubs and leave through the back gate.

Sam "If Dad sees us walk past the house he might want to come."

Billy "Yeah, and he wouldn't want to see how good we are, it might make him feel bad."

Sam "Got anything to eat? I'm pretty hungry."

Billy "I've got some chewing gum in my pocket."

Sam "That'll only make us hungrier.
Chewing gum tricks your stomach.
It gets your juices going and
makes you think you're getting
something to eat."

Billy "Yeah, I heard that
somewhere. Your stomach gets the
message that your jaws are chewing
but no food ever comes down."

Sam "I'll give the gum a miss and get some chips on the way home. Have you ever played golf before?"

Billy "No, but it can't be that hard. Look how easy it is for Tiger Woods. I reckon I'll be pretty good. How about you?"

Sam "Once when Dad was out, I took some of his golf stuff outside and hit a ball off the front lawn. I heard it bounce on a roof up the street."

Billy "So, what did you do?"

Sam "I stuffed the golf club back in his bag and just hoped he wouldn't miss the ball. He had loads anyway!"

CHAPTER 2

Rules Rule

On the way to the park, Billy and Sam plan out the course.

Billy "The sand pit next to the swings can be a bunker."

Sam "And we can start hitting from near the dog mess bin."

Billy "I hope I don't land the ball in dog mess."

Sam "Agh gross!"

Billy "Do you think people should pick up their dog's mess?"

Sam "Yes, it's the law. I'm fed up with treading in it. Our teacher told us that dog mess can make you go blind."

Billy "Yeah, right. As if. So who has to pull the golf buggy around?"

Sam "Well, we could take turns. But why doesn't whoever has to hit the ball next drag the buggy?"

Billy "Nah—in golf, the one who takes the most shots loses, so you'll be dragging the golf bag all the way."

Sam "Want to bet?"

Billy "You're on! Let's see how many hits it takes us to each go to the end of the park and back."

Sam "Well, let's make it that we have to hit that tree at the end of the park before we can turn around. The tree's sort of halfway."

Billy "I wish we'd brought some food with us—I could eat a horse."

Sam "Your stomach never rests. You think more about food than about getting good at golf."

Billy "No I don't. It's just that I need plenty of energy to power through the game ... so I can beat you."

Sam "You'll need more than energy, mate."

CHAPTER 3

Let the Game Begin

It's time for the boys to start the big game. They take all the clubs out of the golf bag and lay them on the ground. Billy picks up the golf club with the wooden end and starts to look at it.

Billy "So what do you call this one?"

Sam "If you don't know that by now how do you think you'll beat me?"

Billy "I'll thrash you just like I thrash you at everything else, because I'm the best."

Sam "In your dreams. You don't even know what the club with the wood on the end is called."

Billy "I do really. I was just testing you to see if you knew what it was."

Sam "So what club are you going to use?"

Sam and Billy shuffle through the golf clubs on the ground. They have a practice swing with each club.

Billy "I think that I might use the one with a 7 on it."

Sam "Why?"

Billy "A 7's on my football shirt and it always works for me in footy."

Sam "Is there a number 30 golf club? That's my favourite number."

Billy "Not here, these clubs only go up to 9."

Sam "Maybe that's why Dad said he isn't playing golf anymore."

Billy "Yeah, maybe his clubs don't go up high enough."

Sam "Well, I'm going to use the club with 3 on it. That's the same as 30 but with the 0 missing."

After a bit of arguing, Sam and Billy work out that they are meant to sit the golf balls on top of the tees. At last the boys are ready to start.

Billy "So who's going first?"
Sam "I should, 'cos it was my idea."

Billy "Well hurry up then, or it will be dark before we finish the game and I'm hungry."

Sam "I reckon I can hit the ball all the way to the tree. Watch out Tiger!"

Billy "I don't think that even Tiger Woods could hit the ball that far."

Sam has a practice swing then walks over to the ball and positions himself. He takes one almighty swing. Both boys look to see where the ball has gone. Billy notices that it's still sitting on the tee.

Sam "That was just a practice swing."

Billy "No it wasn't, you missed the ball. That's your first shot."

Sam takes another swing.

Billy "Mmm, great shot! If you keep
hitting the ball like that, it'll take
you three hundred shots to get to
the tree."

Sam "Okay then, let's see how good
Mr. Hot Shot is."

Billy puts his ball on the tee. He stands behind it with his feet apart then swings. The ball shoots off the tee like a rocket.

Billy "Now that was a great shot."
Sam "Would have been really good if it was straight."

The boys watch as the ball flies
through the air and swerves off to
the right. It heads straight for the
toilet block, thumps into the wall,
ricochets off and torpedos back
towards them. Billy and Sam dive to
the ground just in time to avoid the
ball as it flies over their heads,
barely missing them both.

Sam: "Well, at least my ball went
forward off the tee. Yours is
30 metres behind the tee. If you
keep going like this, the only
way you'll get to the tree is to
go around the park backwards!"

CHAPTER 4

Trouble on the Way

Billy and Sam keep hitting their balls. Each time they watch them land just a few metres in front.

Sam: "Well, between us we've hit the ball more times on one hole than Tiger Woods does in a whole round, even an entire tournament!"

Billy "I reckon it's taken us more hits because our golf clubs are too big."

Sam "I reckon it's because our golf course is too hard. There are a million more obstacles in this park than on any golf course I've seen on TV."

Billy "Well I'm sick of trying to hit the ball at the tree. It's too tall and skinny, like you. I reckon I'll be better at hitting the ball over that pond."

Sam "Better to be tall and skinny than small and stupid. The pond's easy, bags go first."

Billy "Okay Big Mouth, you go first and I'll cheer when you land the ball in the pond."

Sam lines up the ball and hits it as hard as he can. The ball sails high up into the air and then 'plop', lands right in the middle of the pond.

Billy "Woo-hoo! Excellent shot. Lucky you didn't hit a duck."

Sam "Well now we'll see how good you are."

Billy takes a ball out of the golf bag. He lines it up and hits it as hard as he can. 'Plop!' the ball goes into the pond.

Billy "That was a mis-hit. I'm going to have another one. I bet I can hit it over the pond."

Sam "My hit only just missed the other side. I know what I'm doing now so I'm goin' to have another hit too."

Sam and Billy keep trying to get their ball over the pond, but the balls keep landing in the pond. Soon, all the balls in the bag are gone.

"What are you boys doing with my golf clubs?" Sam's father is walking across the park.

Sam "What are we going to say to Dad?"

Billy "Don't know, but you better think fast, especially about how we've just lost all his golf balls."

Sam "Are you a good swimmer?"

Billy "I reckon I should be in the world championships for swimming."

Sam "Good, I think we might be going for a swim to try and find the balls we lost!"

Sam

Golf Lingo

Billy

birdie A score of one hit less than the set number of shots for a hole.

bunker A pit cut into the ground and filled with soft sand. It is difficult to hit a ball out of a bunker.

caddie Someone who carries the clubs for the golfer and looks for their ball.

pit A section of the golf course where a player must hit their ball from the tee to a small hole on the putting green.

hole in one One hit to get the ball straight into the putting green hole!

par The set number of shots it should take you to get the ball in the hole.

33

Golf Must-dos

☞ Make sure that there isn't a sign in the park that says, "Golf practice prohibited". If there is, that means of course that you have to find somewhere else to play.

☞ Make sure that you ask your dad before you use his golf clubs.

☞ Count the number of balls in the golf bag before you start to play. Make sure the same number of golf balls goes back in the bag when you finish playing.

☞ If you are trying to hit a golf ball across a pond make sure there are no ducks on the pond.

☞ Don't hit golf balls anywhere near windows. Glass breaks really easily when you hit it with a golf ball!

☞ If there are people in the park, yell "fore" when you hit the ball so they know it's coming.

☞ If your golf ball lands in dog mess, leave it there.

☞ If you are playing in the park it might be a good idea to wear a helmet.

☞ Most golfers wear shoes with spikes on the bottom to grip the ground. If you don't have golf shoes, you can wear your football boots.

Golf Instant Info

🏌️ The official golf rules were recorded in 1754, in Scotland.

A standard golf course has 18 holes.

The tee is a smoother piece of ground where each player takes their first stoke.

Golf hazards are things such as bunkers, water, or getting your ball stuck in a tree.

The putting green is a carefully prepared grass area where the hole is.

The hole is 10.8 centimetres wide and 10.2 centimetres deep.

Each hole has a flag on a stick that is 2.14 metres long. The flag stick marks where the hole is on the green.

Each player is allowed to use 14 different clubs in a round of golf.

The best thing about playing park golf is trying to hit the ball as far as you can.

Think Tank

1 What is a par?

2 Why do golfers have spikes on the bottom of their shoes?

3 What is a birdie?

4 Why do golfers call "fore"?

5 What are golf buggies are used for?

6 What is the flag on the putting green for?

7 What country does Justin Rose come from?

8 What country is the US Open played in?

Answers

8 The US Open is played in The United States of America.

7 Justin Rose is from England, of course!!

6 The flag shows the golfer where the hole is on the putting green.

5 Golf buggies are used to carry your golf clubs.

4 A golfer calls out "fore" to warn other golfers that a golf ball is heading their way.

3 A birdie is when you score one less than a par.

2 Golfers have spikes on the bottom of their shoes to stop their feet from slipping when they swing at the ball.

1 No, not your father! Each golf hole has a set number of strokes it should take you to get the ball in the hole.

How did you score?

- If you got 8 answers correct, then you might end up being a professional golfer!

- If you got 6 answers correct, maybe you will be able to beat your parents!

- If you got fewer than 4 answers correct, you either have to practise your golf a lot or play football instead.

Felice →   ← Phil

Hi Guys!

We have loads of fun reading and want you to, too. We both believe that being a good reader is really important and so cool.

Try out our suggestions to help you have fun as you read.

At school, why don't you use "Golf Legends" as a play and you and your friends can be the actors. Set the scene for your play. Bring a golf club to school to use as a prop but whatever you do, don't hit a golf ball in the classroom. If you haven't got a golf club, use your acting skills and imagination to pretend.

So ... have you decided who is going to be Billy and who is going to be Sam? Now, with your friends, read and act out our story in front of the class.

We have a lot of fun when we go to schools and read our stories. After we finish the kids all clap really loudly. When you've finished your play your classmates will do the same. Just remember to look out of the window—there might be a talent scout from a television station watching you!

Reading at home is really important and a lot of fun as well.

Take our books home and get someone in your family to read them with you. Maybe they can take on a part in the story.

Remember, reading is a whole lot of fun.

So, as the frog in the local pond would say, Read-it!

And remember, Boys Rule!

Felice

When We Were Kids

Phil

Phil "Did you ever play golf when you were a kid?"

Felice "Yes, I played golf a bit but I was much better at being a caddie."

Phil "Did you ever think you'd be good enough to turn professional?"

Felice "Yeah, only the other day I sent my résumé to Tiger Woods to get a job as a caddie. I'm hoping to get a reply soon."

Phil "Don't hold your breath! I hear Tiger thinks you're too good for him so he might choose someone else!"

BOYZ RULE!
What a Laugh!

Q Why did the golfer wear two pairs of trousers?

A In case he got a hole in one.

BOYS RULE!

Gone Fishing

The Tree House

Golf Legends

Camping Out

Bike Daredevils

Water Rats

Skateboard
Dudes

Tennis Ace

Basketball
Buddies

Secret Agent
Heroes

Wet World

Rock Star

Pirate Attack

Olympic
Champions

Race Car
Dreamers

Hit the Beach

Rotten
School Day

Halloween
Gotcha!

Battle of the
Games

On the Farm